THE PHOENIX CONSPIRACY

'Ella, you are so impatient! We don't know how long it takes to recover from regeneration. It could take months. It's a new kind of treatment. I don't know anyone else who's had it. Do you?'

'No … ' Ella admitted.

'So just try to be patient.'

'OK, but patience isn't my thing.'

More great reads in the SHADES 2.0 series:

THE PHOENIX CONSPIRACY

Mary Chapman

Ransom

SHADES 2.0

The Phoenix Conspiracy

by Mary Chapman

Published by Ransom Publishing Ltd.

Radley House, 8 St. Cross Road, Winchester, Hampshire SO23 9HX, UK

www.ransom.co.uk

ISBN   978 178127 636 5

First published in 2014

CONTENTS

'I'm going to jeek Jake again,' Ella said.
'He's not answered any of our messages.'

She opened her jeeker, pressed *ReadMe*, focusing her mind. The words appeared on the screen as quickly as she thought them:

Jake, plse, plse get back 2 us ...

How R U? ...

We want 2 C U – SOON!! E & R

She pressed *Send*. The words disappeared.

'Leave it for now,' said Ryan. 'You can check it later.'

Ella checked every half-hour. But the screen was still blank long after Ryan had gone home.

The front door banged. It was Ella's mum, home from work. She put her head round the door.

'Haven't you anything better to do than stare at that screen?' she asked.

'I'm waiting to hear from Jake. He's not answering our messages. We've sent loads.'

'Well, he's out of hospital now,' her mum said. 'Didn't you know? I saw him.'

'Where? When?'

'Just now. On my way home. There was an ambulance outside his house. They were carrying him in on a stretcher.'

'A stretcher? Whatever for? He injured his arm, not his legs.'

'He's probably still a bit groggy, after being in hospital so long.'

Ella jumped up. 'I'll go round now.'

Her mum shook her head. 'No. I wouldn't, not today. Leave it until tomorrow, love. He'll be tired. Jeek-speak his mum in the morning and ask her when you can visit.'

'OK, but I can't wait to see him.'

TWO

'His mum was really weird with me,' Ella complained. 'She said he wasn't well enough to see anyone.'

Ryan shrugged. 'Well, he only came home yesterday. And she's probably still angry with us.'

'But it wasn't our fault the chainsaw slipped. It shouldn't have been in their shed anyway.'

'They only kept it because it was his dad's,' Ryan said. 'Like a memento.'

'Yeah, but they should have handed it in like everybody else, years ago, when they made chainsaws illegal.'

Ryan shrugged again. 'His mum will always believe it was our fault he tried to saw that tree down.'

'Don't! I can't bear to remember.'

But she did. She couldn't help it. She remembered ...

... *the almost deafening buzz of the chainsaw ... Jake's screams ... the blade tearing into flesh and bone ... blood spurting ... Jake unable to move, still holding the chainsaw as the blade cut off half his arm ... mangled it so badly it couldn't be sewn on again ...*

'But we're his friends,' she said. 'He'll

want to see us. It's ages since he had the regeneration.'

'It's not ages. You do exaggerate.'

'Whatever. But his mum was weird. Not angry. Something else. I could tell she really didn't want to talk to me. She said to leave it for a week. A *week*!'

'Ella, you are so impatient! We don't know how long it takes to recover from regeneration. It could take months. It's a new kind of treatment. I don't know anyone else who's had it. Do you?'

'No … ' Ella admitted.

'So just try to be patient.'

'OK, but patience isn't my thing.'

'I know,' Ryan grinned.

'I'm longing to see Jake, that's all, because it's so amazing, isn't it, that someone who's lost an arm or a leg can grow it again? Just with an injection of their own stem cells.'

'Yeah. Like a soldier whose leg's been shot off, or a kid who's been knocked off his bike and lost an arm,' Ryan said. 'It's not like in the old days when they were experimenting with cells from human embryos. It's completely different, using the cells from your own body.'

'It's so clever,' Ella said. 'People who've had to have their legs amputated can have them replaced. And if people need new organs, they can grow them now. Just like that. They don't have to wait so long on a transplant list that they die anyway. And people don't have to suffer and be stuck in a wheelchair all their lives, or die really young like they used to.'

'I know. It's great. In a way it sounds simple, but I guess it isn't. Jake probably has to rest a lot, and you're not really very restful, are you?'

Ella smiled. 'Suppose not. But I really will try to be more patient. I'm going to send him a *welcome home* message, though. There's no harm in that, is there?'

A week passed.

But Jake still hadn't replied. And his mum wasn't answering her jeeker.

Ella was losing patience again. 'I'm fed up with this,' she said. 'I'm going round there!'

Ryan sighed. 'You can't just go barging in.'

'Stop being so reasonable. I want to know what's going on. I'm definitely going round to Jake's tomorrow. Otherwise, how are we going to find out what's happening if nobody will tell us?'

THREE

Ella opened her eyes. It was dark.

Her jeeker was glowing, beeping.

She sat up in bed, reached over for it.
Flipped open the lid. Pressed *ReadYou.*

Message from Annabel.

Jake's mum? Then she must have
relented.

But it wasn't from her.

2morro nite. After midnite. Here. J.

That was all. Why was Jake using his mum's jeeker, and not his own?

Midnight.

Jake's house was in darkness.

Ella and Ryan waited in the garden, at the back of the house. But there was no sign of Jake.

'Where is he?' Ella hissed.

Ryan shrugged. 'Probably waiting until his mum's asleep.'

After about an hour, the back door slowly opened. In the sliver of light they could see a figure. It was Jake. He beckoned them, and they followed him, across the lawn, and down to the shed. Once they were inside he carefully closed the door.

'Prop those planks against the window,' he said.

Then he switched on his torch.

'It's so good to see you, even if you have kept us waiting for ages,' said Ella.

She tried to hug him, but he pushed her away.

'What's up with you?' she asked.

'Quite a lot.'

'What's going on, Jake?' asked Ryan. 'Ella's been worried.'

'So've you,' Ella said.

'Just a bit,' said Ryan.

Ella felt really irritated with both of them. Typical boys. Jake had to pretend he wasn't pleased to see her, and Ryan had to pretend he hadn't been worried about Jake. Why couldn't they just be honest about their feelings, like she was?

'Why didn't you answer our messages?' she asked.

'They took my jeeker away,' said Jake.

'Who did? Why? And why wouldn't your mum let us see you?' Ella demanded.

'Is she still mad at us? Does she still blame us?' Ryan asked.

'Yeah … ' Jake hesitated, 'but that's not the main reason.'

'So what is?' Ella asked.

'This.'

He held his torch in his right hand, shining it onto his left arm, the injured one. Then they realised. It stuck out from his body at an odd angle, encased in layers of padding.

'Can you help unwind this bandage stuff?' he asked.

It was difficult to see just by the light of Jake's torch, but between them Ella and Ryan managed to remove the top layers.

'You can stop now,' Jake said. 'And you'd better prepare yourselves.'

FOUR

'What for?' asked Ella. 'Didn't they do the regeneration after all?'

If they hadn't done, she realised she didn't feel ready yet to see the stump of Jake's arm ...

... *the buzz of the chainsaw ... Jake's screams ... her screams ... blood ... splinters of bone sticking out ...*

Jake's voice came through the sounds in her head.

'Yeah, they did it. It was all right at first, after the stem-cell injection, but then – I knew there was something wrong –my arm wasn't growing right.'

Ella's heart thudded. She felt sick. 'What d'you mean?'

Jake put down the torch, unwound the final layers of dressings. His arm still stuck out at a strange angle. He picked up the torch and shone it directly on to his arm.

Except it wasn't an arm. It was nothing like an arm.

It glimmered and glistened in the torchlight. It was widest where it joined Jake's shoulder and then tapered to a point where there should have been a hand, but there wasn't.

Ella shrieked. She covered her eyes with

her hands.

Ryan just stared.

Ella peeped through her fingers. 'What is it?'

Ryan made a sort of croaky sound. He was trying to speak but couldn't. He coughed and tried again.

'I think … ' he coughed again. 'I think it's a flipper,' he said.

Ella slowly took her hands away from her face.

'It's got feathers, like a wing,' Ella said. She still felt sick.

'Jake, whatever have they done to you?' Ryan asked.

'I don't know. As soon as this started growing, they put me into isolation. Loads of doctors examined me, whispering to each other as though I wasn't there. Mum was crying … '

'Jake, sorry ... ' Ella gasped, 'but can you cover it up, please? I'm sorry, but it's gross.'

'OK.' He loosely wrapped the dressings round the flipper.

'What happened then?' asked Ryan.

'They sent me home with a nurse – to monitor me, as they call it. Guard me is more like it. She keeps watch all the time. At night she sleeps in the next room. She's been giving me a pill that completely knocks me out. Said it was for the pain. Tonight I managed to pretend to swallow it and then spit it out as soon as she left the room. But it was ages before she settled down. I could hear her moving about. That's why I was late getting out. She makes sure I don't have any visitors, and she watches Mum as well. Mum had to sign a document at the hospital about confidentiality before they would let me come home.'

'Do you know why it went wrong?' Ella asked.

'They said they thought the stem cells might have been contaminated. Whatever that means. How, or by what, they didn't say. There's an investigation going on. Mum and I have been forbidden to speak to anyone about it. But I was desperate to tell you, so I managed to sneak that message on Mum's jeeker. I deleted it straightaway, just in case.'

'What are they doing about your arm?' Ella asked.

'They've stopped the drugs I was taking to help re-growth. I've got to wait and see if this flipper thing will wither away.'

'Then what?'

'They'll try again, but they said it mightn't work.'

Ella looked at Jake in horror. 'But that's terrible.'

Jake nodded. 'Yeah, I know. So I want to find out what went wrong. How it happened. So it doesn't happen again. But I can't get away from here. I need your help. I've worked it all out. This is what I want you to do.'

FIVE

The Phoenix Hospital was two bus journeys away, on the far side of town.

Ella and Ryan decided beforehand that they would arrive during visiting hours when there were lots of people around.

It was a sunny day. Several patients were walking in the grounds with their visitors.

Ella stared at them.

'Do you think *their* regenerations worked all right?'

'They wouldn't let them out if they hadn't. Come on, let's find the lab. It's probably at the back of the main block.'

They walked across the lawns in front of the hospital, pausing now and again, pretending to admire the roses. Once round the corner of the building they started to hurry. The path wound through a shrubbery of bushes and small trees, so they were hidden from anyone in the building or the grounds.

Ahead was a sign:

LABORATORIES:
NO PUBLIC ACCESS
ALL PERSONNEL
REPORT TO SECURITY

Ella sighed. 'There's more than one lab, then. I wonder which one we want?'

'Let's have a look through that window,' said Ryan.

They left the path, moved closer to the building and crouched down.

Ryan glanced up at the window.

'Triple-glazed. We won't be able to hear anything.'

'We'll have to risk a quick peep.' Ella slowly raised her head just above the level of the windowsill. 'Nobody there,' she whispered.

They both peered in.

It was the security guard's office. On the wall facing them were rows of CCTV screens, showing people moving around in different parts of the hospital. Each vertical row of screens was labelled:

SALAMANDER LAB
STAFF LOCKER ROOM
CRICK LAB

WARDS 1, 2, 3, 4

'So there *are* two labs,' Ryan said.
'Salamander and Crick.'

'Look, there's somebody in the
Salamander lab.' Ella held her jeeker up to
the window.

'Ready to record?' Ryan asked.

'Yeah. I've set it on low light and
maximum magnification.'

'Great. Make sure you record everything.'

'Do you want to do it?'

'No. I was just saying. This could be our
only chance.'

The CCTV screen labelled
SALAMANDER LAB showed a room. The
walls were lined with rows of shiny white
cabinets, all labelled, each about half a
metre square. A white-suited, masked and
gloved figure stopped in front of one of the
cabinets. The door sprang open.

'They must have an iris recognition security system,' Ella said.

The figure – small and slim, probably female – swiftly removed a pack from the cabinet and put it into the small metal case she was carrying. A cloud of mist swirled out before the door closed.

'Those cabinets must be freezers,' Ryan said, 'storing stem cells.'

The figure disappeared from the screen. Then reappeared on another screen labelled STAFF LOCKER ROOM, placed the pack in a locker and disappeared again.

Almost immediately, a taller, broader figure, probably male, wearing the same uniform, came into the room and strode over to the locker. While he was removing the pack another white-suited figure came in and nodded in his direction in a friendly sort of way, as if he knew him. The man nodded back, quickly put the pack into a metal case identical to the one they'd seen earlier, and left the room.

They tracked his progress from screen to screen, to the CRICK LAB, identical to the SALAMANDER LAB, with small cabinets – all presumably freezers holding individual packs of frozen stem cells.

They watched the man as he carefully peeled the label off the pack, stuck on another label, selected a freezer, waited until the door opened, and thrust the pack inside. He stepped back and the door of the freezer closed.

At that moment someone else came into the lab, and the man they'd been watching moved quickly away from the freezer and hurried out of the room.

Ella's arm ached with holding her jeeker steady against the windowpane. Her legs were stiff with crouching. Neither she nor Ryan heard the man in uniform creeping up behind them.

Ryan felt a hand on his shoulder.

'What d'you think you're doing?'

It was the security guard. He made a grab for Ella as well, but she was already on her feet, closing her jeeker.

'Go! Go!' Ryan shouted.

For a moment she couldn't move.

'Go on!'

She ran.

When she reached the corner of the building she glanced quickly over her shoulder. Ryan was still struggling with the security guard. She was puzzled. Why hadn't he got away? He was brilliant at judo.

Then she realised. He was deliberately letting the guard keep hold of him so she could escape with the evidence.

The best thing she could do was to keep running, and get as far away from the hospital as possible. She'd have to hope that nobody would come to help the guard, and that Ryan would be able to make his getaway.

SIX

Her jeeker bleeped. Ryan was home. Great!
They could stick to their plan to go to
Jake's at midnight and show him what
they'd discovered.

'What can we use as a screen?' Ella asked,
shining her torch round the shed.
   'There's some old dust sheets somewhere

in here that my dad used when he was painting,' Jake said.

'Could they be in here?' Ryan dragged a plastic sack out from behind the lawnmower and tipped out the contents. 'Yeah, they are.'

Ella held the sheet up against the back wall of the shed, while Ryan knocked in a few nails to hold it up.

'That'll do.'

'Not bad,' Jake said, as Ella projected the magnified images onto their make-do screen. 'The magnification's really good.'

'You can even read the freezer labels,' Ryan said. 'In the first lab they're labelled SAL for Salamander, I guess, and in the second CRI for Crick.'

'I can make out some other words,' Ella said. '*Peter Aston ... leg. Andrew Johnson ... arm. Juliet Swallow ... kidney* – that's creepy.'

'It doesn't mean there are people's actual arms, legs or kidneys in there,' Jake said, 'just their stem cells.'

'I know *that*, but it's still weird,' Ella said. 'And, look, there are numbers as well.'

'Don't let's bother with those now,' said Ryan. 'Let's look at that frame of the Staff Locker Room. There might be a name on the locker.'

There wasn't a name, but there were initials – *JT*.

'That's odd,' Ryan said. 'When we were at the hospital, watching on the CCTV screens, we definitely saw two different people using the same locker. But surely everybody would have their own locker, with their own initials on it?'

'Mmm,' Ella thought for a moment. 'Let's see the bit where the second person peels the label off the pack. If we could read what it says on each of the labels – '

'I can see the words on the new label,' Jake said. '*Lower leg. Adult male. Jon M Dawson Hosp. Reg. 22348. CRI 09/08/2025* – that must be the date it was frozen.'

'Look, the first label – the one that was peeled off the pack – is down there, on the ground,' Ella said. 'Don't you remember, someone else came into the lab, and you could tell the guy we were watching was in a hurry to get away as fast as he could? He must have dropped the label without realising it. Oh, please let it be the right way up.'

It was. And they could read it, even though it was creased and crumpled:

Mature Shark's Fin. SAL 09/08/2025.

'Same date!' Ryan tried to keep his voice low. 'Jon Dawson's going to end up with a shark's fin instead of a leg!'

'That's what must have happened to me,' Jake said slowly. 'Someone swapped my human stem cells for non-human ones.'

'So it wasn't an accident,' Ella said. 'It was deliberate.'

'The trouble is, we can't identify who did it.'

For a few moments they were silent, hardly able to believe what they had discovered.

Then Ryan spoke. 'Those initials, on that locker, JT. Maybe the two people we saw have the same initials, so they can use the same locker without anyone getting suspicious. But who are they?'

'We could look it up,' Jake said. 'See if we can track them down. A few years ago there was loads about regeneration therapy. Lots of people didn't want it to happen. Said it was unnatural. I think there was

actually an Anti-Regeneration Movement
…'

'Yeah, I remember,' Ryan said. 'They called it ARM. There were marches and protests. But after the Regeneration Act was passed last year it all went quiet.'

Ella had been busy on her jeeker. 'You're right. Here's the official ARM site. Maybe there's a member of ARM with the initials JT. There's an Open Forum here. Let's check that.'

There were twenty or so messages posted on the Forum. No full names. Just initials.

'There!' Ryan pointed. '*JT* – but it's got a number one after it. That must be a code name.'

'There are lots of messages from JT1,' Jake said.

' *… unnatural … irreligious … against God's laws … up to every individual to protest*

… we must all, each and every one of us, make a stand against these immoral practices … a matter of conscience … must take action …'

'He's wound up, isn't he? If it is a he.' Ryan pointed the screen, 'And look. Here's JT2, exchanging messages with JT1.'

' … unethical … must make a stand … individual conscience … direct action … essential … not enough research done into the side-effects or long-term effects of regeneration … everyone will want regeneration for all their body parts … against the natural order … "a time to be born, and a time to die" … everyone will live longer… over-population … famine …'

'Well, they obviously agree with each other!' Ella said. 'But look, these messages were posted last year, and then they stop.'

'Maybe they were too extreme for ARM,'

Jake said. 'Maybe they set up something else.'

'Let's try putting in Anti-Regeneration and Direct Action,' Ella said.

And there they were – JT1 and JT2, founder members of DAAR: Direct Action Against Regeneration.

'They still don't give their full names,' Jake said, 'but they say they have qualifications in medicine and in stem-cell therapy.'

'So supposing they both got jobs in the labs at Phoenix Hospital,' Ryan said, 'one in Salamander and one in Crick? And because they've the same initials – JT – like I said, they can use the same locker in the Locker Room without anybody wondering why. That's their drop.'

'Like spies,' Ella said.

'They're fanatics,' Jake said. His voice

was very serious. 'They're dangerous.'

'Have we got enough evidence against them?' Ryan asked.

'I think so,' Ella said. 'But who can we tell?'

SEVEN

'We can't tell anyone at the hospital,' Jake
said. 'We don't know who JT1 and JT2 are,
and we don't know who else there is against
regeneration. I wouldn't trust my nurse, for
instance.'

'But if we don't tell someone this'll keep
happening,' Ryan said. 'Then one day the
Anti-Regenerationists will leak the story of

failed regenerations to the media. That must be what they plan to do. It'll be a scandal. The Government will decide regeneration doesn't work and stop it. And the Anti-Regenerationists will have succeeded.'

'That would be terrible,' Ella said. 'All those ill or wounded people, looking forward to leading normal lives again through regeneration. And then suddenly that hope is snatched way by these Anti-Regenerationists. They're *still* protesting, even though these days stem cells are taken from the patients' own body tissues, not from fertilised human eggs. I know lots of people were against stem-cell research when they used human embryos. I can understand why some people didn't agree with that. But it's done differently now.'

'I know,' Ryan said. 'One of their

objections seems to be that it's unnatural, whatever *that* means. And yet they are using stem cells themselves, from sharks and penguins and goodness know what else. That's unnatural if anything is, and I bet they don't get the shark's consent.'

'No, I bet they don't,' Ella said. 'I know that's a joke, but in a way it's true. They say what other people do is immoral, but they do just the same things when it suits them. And I bet none of *them* needs a new arm or leg, or anyone they care about. If they did they might think differently. We can't let them do this.'

'But how can we stop them?' Jake asked.

'We've got to tell somebody right at the top,' Ella said, 'somebody who's really committed to regeneration.'

There was a silence. Then Ryan spoke.

'I'm beginning to wonder if we've got a

bit carried away, and whether anybody'll believe us. We're just three teenagers,' he said. 'So who's going to take notice of us? All we've got is a bit of video, showing two people who we think both have the initials JT, and who may be the same as JT1 and JT2 on those websites. It's a bit thin.'

'Well, yeah, but we mustn't give up,' Jake said. 'Let's look up some more and see if we can find out who's been involved from the start, since the first regeneration experiments. There just has to be someone out there we can tell.'

It took a long time, but in the end they narrowed it down to two names, both strong supporters of regeneration, and at the forefront of research. Professor Angus Wheatley and Professor Claire French were both heads of Stem Cell Research Centres.

Ryan stared at the screen. 'There's nothing to choose between them.'

'No. They've both been on all the important committees, and written loads of articles and books about stem cells,' Jake said. 'So let's jeek them both.'

'That's a good idea,' Ryan said.

They discussed what to put in the jeek so it was clear in Ella's mind. Then she pressed *ReadMe* and focused on the screen, transferring her thoughts and the CCTV images to her jeeker.

At last she was ready, finger poised over *Send*.

'Shall I do it now?'

Ryan grabbed her hand just in time. 'No! You need to enter the anonymity code, or they'll trace it back to your jeeker.'

'Sorry! Sorry! I forgot.'

She focused again on the screen. It

darkened and then brightened.

'OK now,' Ryan said.

Ella pressed *Send*.

EIGHT

Professor Angus Wheatley leaned back in his First Class seat on Flight EA0039. He was looking forward to being one of the key speakers at the Hong Kong Conference.

This year's theme was *Regeneration: the Next Phase*. He had plenty of ideas about how to take regeneration forward into the future. In fact, he was already on to something new, which would revolutionise medicine. Then he should finally get his just reward ...

... the Nobel Prize for Medicine goes to ... (pause) ... Professor Angus Wheatley ... (applause).

He smiled to himself. A fantasy now, but soon it would be reality.

And while he was away his new super-efficient secretary, Alison, would look after the office. He could leave everything in her capable hands. In the few months she'd been with him, she'd shown she was absolutely trustworthy. He needn't waste time now on trivial things like checking his jeeks. Alison was perfectly capable of dealing with them all. He could concentrate on more important things. He closed his eyes ...

... and the Nobel Prize for Medicine goes to

... (*pause*) ... *Professor Angus Wheatley* ... (*applause*).

In Professor Wheatley's office, Alison Fraser sat at the professor's desk.

It was the first time he had been away since she started working for him. She smiled to herself. Before he left for Hong Kong, he'd told her she was the best secretary he'd ever had and that he had absolute confidence in her.

It was time to check his jeeks. She opened his jeeker.

Beep, beep ...

She pressed *ReadYou*.

Evidence of sabotage of regeneration therapy at Phoenix Hospital ...

What was this?

She read the jeek, and then looked at the attached images. Who on Earth had sent them, and how had they got hold of them?

Professor Wheatley mustn't see this.

Alison sank back in the chair, going over recent events at the Phoenix Hospital in her mind – the case of the boy with the flipper. Thank goodness the hospital's internal investigation into the possible contamination of stem cells wouldn't reveal anything. JT1 and JT2 would make sure of that.

JT1 – James Tilford, her brother – was Chair of the Enquiry. JT2 – Judith Thompson – was Chief Investigator. Between them they'd keep the lid on things.

All the members of DAAR knew it was imperative that their sabotage programme wasn't stopped at this stage. They needed another ten months or so to intervene in more regeneration treatments. Then they'd have the evidence – or so it would appear to everyone – that in over 50% of cases regeneration fails.

Nobody would suspect that James or Judith, or their associates in DAAR, had brought about these results through their own secret actions.

The public would completely lose faith in regeneration therapy. It would be removed from the Register of the International Institute of Approved Cures and Treatments. It would be banned. Everything would have gone according to plan.

Alison smiled and pressed *DeleteYou*.

She sat back in her chair with a satisfied sigh. She was only a small cog in the machine, but she'd done her bit. In the short time she'd been working for Professor Wheatley she'd won his complete confidence. He thought she was as committed to regeneration as he was.

But he wasn't as clever as he thought he was. He had no idea he had a traitor in his office. Now nobody would ever know about DAAR's sabotage – thanks to her!

Professor Claire French leaned back in her seat (Economy Class) on Flight EA0039 to Hong Kong. She opened her jeeker to have a final look at her lecture notes. She was the first speaker tomorrow morning.

Beep, beep …

She pressed *ReadYou*.

Evidence of sabotage of regeneration therapy at Phoenix Hospital …

She read the jeek and looked at the attached images. This was terrible!

It all made sense now. She'd had an uneasy feeling on her last visit to the Phoenix Hospital. Some of the research staff had seemed reluctant for her to look round the labs.

She couldn't ignore this information. Even if it was anonymous. She couldn't keep it to herself. She must take action. But how?

She gazed out of the window, looking down on the clouds, trying to think calmly. Who should she tell when she got back from Hong Kong? Who could she trust? Maybe, instead of telling one or two individuals, it would be better to tell as many people as possible, simultaneously.

She smiled. Of course! She had a ready-made audience. A global one. The Hong Kong Conference was the ideal place for her to expose the plan to sabotage regeneration therapy. She would show these images in her presentation. She must make sure everyone, including the media, recognised how far opponents of regeneration were prepared to go, and how nearly they had succeeded.

Although they were scientists, they were fanatics. Criminals in fact, highly organised and committed to their cause. They must be found and punished, but most important of all, stopped.

If this information hadn't reached her ... she couldn't bear to think what might have happened. She shivered at the thought of how close total failure had been. All those years of painstaking research wasted. All those people doomed to suffer illness, disability, death.

Of course, she must remember that in the early days of research into adult stem cells she herself had had some doubts. She'd worried whether she and her colleagues were trying to play God. But none of them had been doing their work for profit. All of them had wanted to relieve human suffering and improve the quality of people's lives.

And once they had begun the trials involving human patients, using their own stem cells, then all her doubts had disappeared.

She started to re-write the opening paragraphs of her lecture.

NINE

Six months later, Jake, home from hospital, proudly showed Ella and Ryan his new arm.

'Grown from my own stem cells,' he said. 'Nobody swapped them this time!'

Ella grinned. 'Much as I like penguins, I'm glad you didn't turn into one!'

'You can laugh now,' Ryan said. 'But it wasn't a joke, Ella.'

'I know that, but it's just such a relief. Jake's complete again, and those Anti-Regenerationists are all behind bars now. It's a pity nobody knows we put them there.'

'But we know we did it. That's what matters,' Jake said.

'And really it's better nobody knows,' Ryan said. 'Just in case some of their supporters are still out there. It's safer for us to be anonymous.'

'I hadn't thought of that.' Ella shivered.

'Yeah, Ryan's right,' Jake said. 'We are safer if nobody knows.'

Meanwhile, in Professor Wheatley's office Alison Fraser sat at the professor's desk. He was away again, at another conference. She sipped her coffee and gazed out of the window.

Of course, she thought, it was a great

shame about James and Judith and everyone in DAAR. Obviously several years in prison wasn't a step up in their careers. But then lots of people had written books about their experiences 'inside', and it hadn't done their careers any harm. Quite the opposite. And, anyway, sacrifices have to be made.

She had been rather clever, she thought. Being a small cog in the machine, just a secretary, it was easy to be overlooked. Nobody had realised that she, Alison Fraser, was related to James Tilford. Because of her married name, no one knew James was her brother.

And there was something else they didn't know. She was really a scientist herself, not just a secretary. Of course, she was a brilliant secretary, just as she was a brilliant scientist. She'd studied medicine abroad, and then done research into stem-cell therapy, moving around every couple of years, from country to country.

And that was when she'd made contacts with pharmaceutical firms, and when she'd realised how much they had to lose if stem-cell therapy really took off. If damaged organs, tissues and limbs could be regenerated, and strokes, diabetes, heart disease and blindness could be treated by stem-cell therapy, then nobody would need drugs.

Drugs only treated the symptoms. But stem cells could cure you. Pharmaceutical firms wanted to protect their profits and their shareholders. They were prepared to pay a huge amount of money to someone like herself, expert enough to sabotage developments in stem-cell therapy. Or regenerative medicine, as some people preferred to call it.

She wasn't a bit concerned, like James and Judith, or those other fanatics in DAAR, about what was natural or not. All their religious and moral objections didn't bother her in the slightest. But it suited her to go along with them, and they'd served their purpose.

Now she would go it alone, but with plenty of financial backing. At first she would watch and wait. She was in an ideal position as Professor Wheatley's secretary. She was at the very centre, the hub, the cutting edge.

Every piece of information about the very latest developments passed through her hands, and also about the research scientists themselves. She had ways and means of finding out about their personal lives, their weaknesses, as well as their professional strengths.

So she could get to know who she could put pressure on to join her 'team'. Or rather, one of her teams. Because there were two, and neither knew of the other's existence. That was what was so clever.

The job of one team was to prove that regeneration was totally bad, and that drugs were best. The pharmaceutical firms would pay her thousands and thousands of pounds for this service.

The job of her other team was secretly to provide regeneration to the very rich, and only the very rich – only those who could afford to pay her thousands and thousands of pounds for such an exclusive service.

What had happened to James and Judith was not the end of it, but the beginning of a new phase. She was in charge this time, and this time there would be no mistakes.

There was just one thing. One slight niggling worry. She still didn't know who had sent that jeek, the one she'd deleted, and the one sent to Professor Claire French. Was it an individual? No, more likely it was a group.

Scientists? Or one of those dreadful patients' rights groups. As if patients could possibly know what was best for them.

Watch and wait, that's what she must do. She was good at that.

Once she knew who her enemies were, she would deal with them.

Virus

by Mary Chapman

Every aspect of Penna's life is controlled for her: a computer programme tells her when to get up, when to eat, even when to sleep. It's the same for everybody in this brave new world. But one day the programme goes wrong and suddenly everybody is on their own. Could it be part of some big plan?

Danger Money

by Mary Chapman

As a World War One recruit onboard the fishing boat the *Admiral*, all Bob Thompson can think about is how much he will earn. Bob gets danger money, as the ship defends itself against German subs. But by the time Bob realises what he has taken on, it's too late to go back.